NINJA
NAN

This edition published in 2016
by Scholastic Children's Books Euston House, 24 Eversholt Street, London NW1 1DB
a division of Scholastic Ltd
www.scholastic.co.uk
London · New York · Toronto · Sydney · Auckland · Mexico City · New Delhi · Hong Kong

PB ISBN 978 1407 15530 2
 • Printed in Malaysia

1 3 5 7 9 10 8 6 4 2

NINJA NAN
Follow your dreams!
Written by
Hollie Hughes
Illustrated by
Natalie Smillie
SCHOLASTIC

My nan has always been an ordinary, everyday kind of nan.

By day she knits big baggy jumpers,
and long woolly socks.

By night, she plays
card games with
her friends.

But all that changed when, one day,
I found a note stuck to the fridge:

Dear Jim,

I am running away to join the circus.

I know this will be a shock to you, but sometimes a nan's just gotta do what a nan's gotta do.

I'll always be your nan, and I love you very much. Please come and visit me at the circus.

Love, Nan (Ninja Nan)

Ninja Nan!

What on earth was **Nan** doing at the circus?

Luckily, the next day was a Saturday – so I begged Mum to take me to visit Nan.

Mum tutted and shook her head, and said Nan had 'some serious growing up to do,' but she said yes in the end.

When we arrived at the circus, Nan was waiting inside the Big Top. She waved excitedly before whisking us off on a tour. The first person she took us to meet was Harry Hercules, the ringmaster.

Your nan is **awesome**! I've never seen a talent like it – she's going to be the **star** of the show!

Nan beamed as Harry Hercules unveiled her brand new poster . . .

HARRY HERCULES
AND HIS HAIR-RAISING CIRCUS
ARE PROUD TO PRESENT
THE ONE AND ONLY
NINJA NAN
COME AND SEE THE AMAZING
JUGGLING, WEIGHTLIFTING
TIGHTROPE-WALKING, ACROBATIC
SUPERSTAR NINJA
FOR YOURSELF!

Mum looked worried.

"Weightlifting?
Tightrope walking?"

she gasped.

"It's fine," said Nan.
"I'm a **professional** now."

"Come on," called Nan. "I've got **loads** to show you – just wait till you see my **caravan**!"

"Hmm," said Mum.
"We'll have to see about that . . ."

Next, Nan took us to see all the other performers.

There were **contortionists** tying themselves up in knots,

strongmen lifting strongmen,

jugglers on horseback,

ballroom-dancing **dogs**,

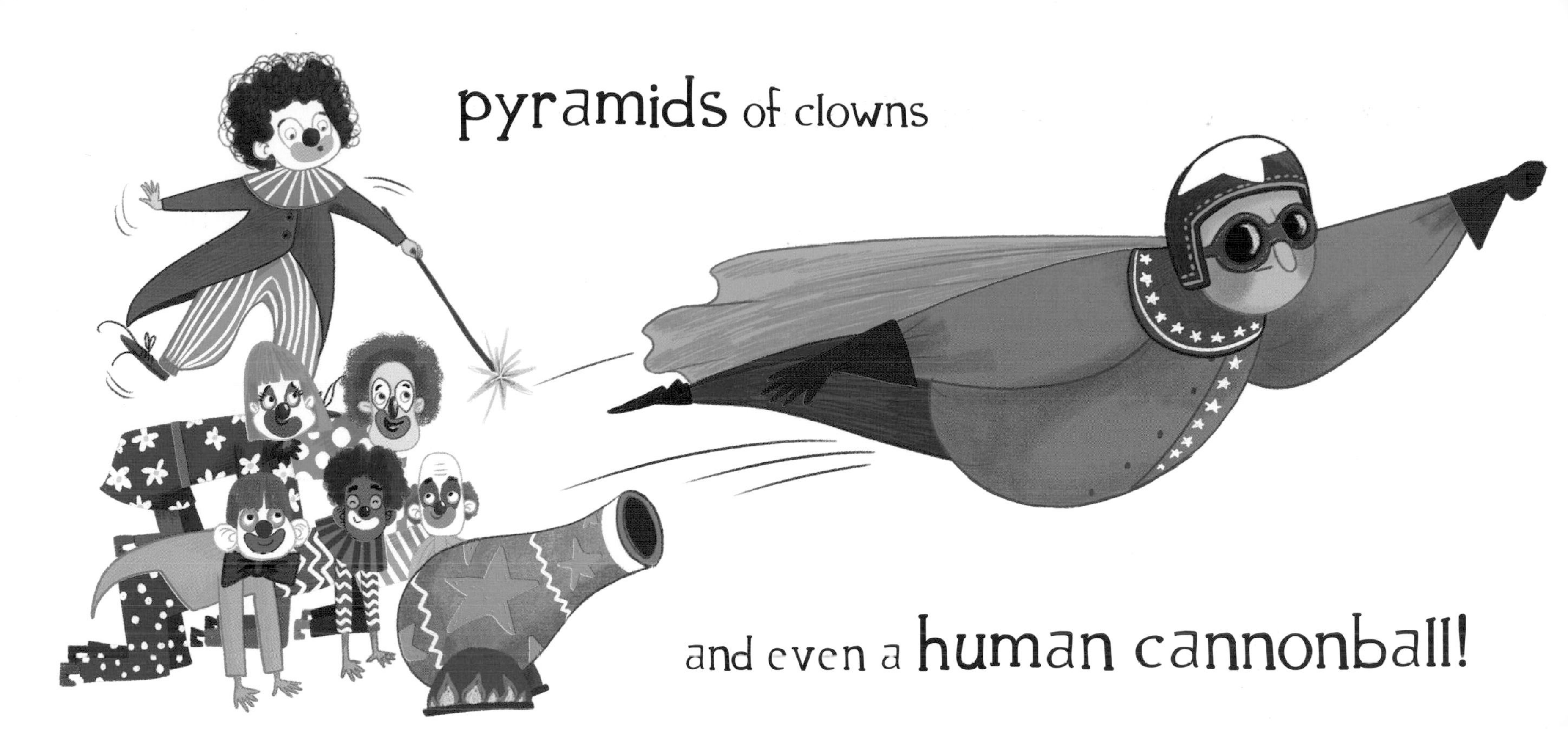

pyramids of clowns

and even a **human cannonball!**

My absolute favourites were Clunky the Clown and The Flying Pigs. Even Mum had to admit she liked those and, because she was being very good, Pedro the Pigman let her hold the baby of the family for a cuddle.

Finally, it was time for the show.
I could feel Mum shaking in the seat next to me,
so I took her hand and gave it a squeeze.

We had seats in the very front row because Nan was the STAR! Mum wasn't too happy when Clunky the Clown squirted us with water though.

Harry Hercules
cracked his whip
and on came act
after act,

THE BRILLIANT BRUTUS BROTHERS

The GREAT SPINDERELLA

each more
jaw-dropping
than the
one before.

MADAME VOLANTE

Mum and I were on the edge of our seats, waiting and waiting for Nan to come out.

PEDRO AND THE FLYING PIGS

01

Until, at last, it was time for the

grand finale.

Nan looked stunning – just like a

real Ninja!

Wow! What an act!
The poster had said that Nan would be
weightlifting and doing acrobatics. . .

. . . but she was doing everything at the same time, whilst swinging from the trapeze! The crowd went wild, cheering and shouting, "Ninja Nan, Ninja Nan!"
And that was just the start . . .

Suddenly, there was a **FLASH** and a booming **BANG.**

Everyone went quiet as all the lights went out and the Big Top was plunged into darkness.

Moments later, a spotlight showed Nan wobbling on a tightrope, high above Harry Hercules and the crowd below.

Harry lit the cannon and started to fire sparkly balloons high into the air.
I gasped – was Nan going to fall?
But instead, with a **huge Ninja shout...**

Nan took a flying leap off the tightrope, knitting needles
flashing as she popped every balloon on her way down.
Even Mum looked impressed.

After the show was over, Nan bought me a hot dog and a great big cloud of pink candyfloss. We sat on deckchairs outside her caravan – chatting and chomping cheerfully.

"Wow!" I said. "Nan, you *are* **amazing** – I can't believe I ever thought you were ordinary. And Mum will be proud too, you know – once she gets used to the idea."

"Thank you Jim," said Nan. "I knew you'd understand."

"Suppose we'd better go and see where she's got to then," I said . . .

WONDER MUM

Mum?
YING PIGS

REMEMBER KIDS

NAN IS A HIGHLY TRAINED CIRCUS PROFESSIONAL. ALL OF HER ACTS ARE EXTREMELY DANGEROUS, AND MUST NOT BE TRIED AT HOME.

No animals or nans were harmed in the making of this book.